Alice in Wonderland & Through the Looking-Glass

Retold from the Lewis Carroll originals by Eva Mason

Illustrated by Dan Andreasen

STERLING CHILDREN'S BOOKS
New York

STERLING CHILDREN'S BOOKS
New York

An Imprint of Sterling Publishing
387 Park Avenue South
New York, NY 10016

STERLING CHILDREN'S BOOKS and the distinctive Sterling Children's Books logo
are trademarks of Sterling Publishing Co., Inc.

Text © 2009 by Eva Mason
Illustrations © 2009 by Dan Andreasen

All rights reserved. No part of this publication may be reproduced, stored in a retrieval system, or transmitted, in any
form or by any means, electronic, mechanical, photocopying, recording, or otherwise, without prior written permission
from the publisher.

ISBN 978-1-4027-9467-4

Distributed in Canada by Sterling Publishing
c/o Canadian Manda Group, 165 Dufferin Street
Toronto, Ontario, Canada M6K 3H6
Distributed in the United Kingdom by GMC Distribution Services
Castle Place, 166 High Street, Lewes, East Sussex, England BN7 1XU
Distributed in Australia by Capricorn Link (Australia) Pty. Ltd.
P.O. Box 704, Windsor, NSW 2756, Australia

Classic Starts is a trademark of Sterling Publishing Co., Inc.

For information about custom editions, special sales, and premium and corporate purchases, please contact Sterling
Special Sales at 800-805-5489 or specialsales@sterlingpublishing.com.

Printed in China
Lot #:
4 6 8 10 9 7 5 3
06/13

LONDON BOROUGH OF SUTTON LIBRARY SERVICE	
30119 027 533 54 8	
Askews & Holts	Aug-2014
JF	

CONTENTS

Alice in Wonderland

Through the Looking-Glass

Alice in Wonderland

CHAPTER 1

Down the Rabbit Hole

Alice was getting so very bored sitting with her sister on the riverbank. She had nothing to do. She was just wondering if making a daisy chain was worth the trouble of getting up to pick the daisies when she saw a rabbit in a waistcoat.

"Oh, dear! I'll be late!" cried the White Rabbit.

Alice didn't think it was strange that the Rabbit was talking to himself. But she did find it odd when the Rabbit took a watch out of his coat pocket. She had never seen a rabbit with a watch, much less a pocket in which to keep it.

Alice was burning with curiosity. Before her sister could stop her, she ran after the White Rabbit. He hopped into a large rabbit hole and she jumped in after him.

And then she was falling. And falling.

Down, down, down. Would the fall *never* end?

There was nothing else to do, so Alice talked aloud to herself. "Dinah will miss me very much tonight," she said. Dinah was Alice's cat. "Dinah, my dear, I wish you were down here with me! There are no mice in the air, I'm afraid. But you might catch a bat. And a bat is like a mouse. But do cats eat bats, I wonder?"

Alice was getting sleepy. The fall was just so very long. She mumbled, "Do cats eat bats? Do cats eat bats?" And sometimes, "Do bats eat cats?" She couldn't answer either question, so it didn't really matter *which* way she said it.

Suddenly . . . *thump!* She had landed on a pile of dry leaves. The fall was over.

Alice was not hurt one bit. Up ahead, she saw the White Rabbit hurrying down a long hallway. She ran after him, but lost him around a corner.

There were doors all around her, but every single one was locked. Alice felt so sad. She had come all this way and had lost the Rabbit. And, worse, now she was stuck.

Then she noticed a small glass table. On top was a tiny golden key. When she turned around, she saw a little door that hadn't been there before. It was about fifteen inches high. To her delight, the key fit the lock perfectly!

The door opened onto a passage the size of a rat hole. Alice got on her knees to peek through. What she saw was the most lovely garden ever. She wanted to reach the colorful flowers, but not even her head could fit into the tiny doorway.

It was no use. Alice went back to the little table and set the key down. Now there was a tiny bottle on the table. She was sure it hadn't been there before. On the bottle were the words DRINK ME.

Alice was far too wise to drink a bottle just because it told her to. She knew she should see first if it was marked POISON.

This bottle was not marked POISON, which meant that she could drink it. And drink it she did.

"What a curious feeling!" Alice cried.

Curious indeed. Alice was shrinking. In the blink of an eye, she was only ten inches high. Now she could go into the garden!

But poor Alice. When she went to the tiny door, she found it locked again. And when she went to get the key, she discovered that she was far too small to reach it on top of the table.

She sat down on the floor and cried.

"There's no use crying!" Alice scolded herself. She liked to pretend to be two people. *But there's no use pretending to be two people now,* she thought. *There's hardly enough of me left to make* one *whole person!*

Just then her eyes fell on a little glass box under the table. In it was a small cake. The words EAT ME were written on the top in raisins.

"Well, I'll eat it!" said Alice. "If it makes me grow larger, I can reach the key. If it makes me grow smaller, I can creep under the door. Either way, I'll get into the garden!"

Alice took the tiniest bite. "Which way?" she said to herself, and was quite surprised to find that she was still the same size. This is usually what happens when one eats cake, but Alice was by now used to strange things happening. It seemed dull for nothing to happen at all.

So she took another bite. Soon she had eaten the entire cake.

CHAPTER 2

The Pool of Tears

❦

"Curiouser and curiouser!" Alice said. She was now growing toward the ceiling.

"Good-bye, feet!" she added. She could barely see them anymore. "Oh, my poor little feet. I wonder who will put on your shoes and socks now?"

Alice kept growing. She wondered how she would get a new pair of shoes to her feet now that she could no longer reach them. They were so very far away that she decided she would have to mail them. As she thought this, her head hit the ceiling. She was more than nine feet tall. She quickly grabbed the golden key and hurried for the garden door.

Poor Alice! She was far too huge to fit through it *now*. All she could do was lie down and peek into the garden with one eye. Of course she began to cry again.

"You should be ashamed!" she scolded herself. "A big girl like you crying this way!"

It didn't help. She kept crying, shedding gallons of tears. Soon there was a large pool on the floor. It was about four inches deep and reached halfway down the hall.

Then she heard footsteps. It was the White Rabbit. He had dressed up in a fancy suit and was carrying white gloves and a large fan. As he hurried along, he muttered, "Oh, the Duchess! She'll be *awful* if I keep her waiting . . ."

"If you please, sir—" Alice called to him.

The Rabbit jumped at her voice. In fact, he

was so startled, he dropped his fan and gloves and then ran away, leaving them behind.

Alice picked up the fan and the white gloves. The hallway was so very hot. She started to fan her face, talking to herself as she did. "How strange everything is today! I wonder if I was changed in the night? Let me think. *Was* I the same when I got up this morning? I think I remember feeling a little different. But if I'm not me, the next question is: Who in the world *am* I? *That's* the puzzle!"

She thought about all the other children she knew. She couldn't be Ada because Ada's hair was curly. She couldn't be Mabel because she knew lots of things and Mabel knew very little.

"Besides," Alice said, "she's *she,* and I'm *I.* Oh, how confusing! I should see if I know all the things I used to know. Let's see, four times five is twelve. And four times six is thirteen. And four times seven is—oh, dear! I'll never get to twenty that way. Let's try geography. London is the capital of Paris. And Paris is the capital of Rome—no, that's wrong! I *must* be Mabel!"

She tried to recite a poem she knew, but her voice sounded rough and strange in her throat. And the words came out all wrong.

Alice's eyes filled with tears again. "If I'm Mabel, I'll stay down here forever!" she said. As she said this, she noticed she was wearing one of the Rabbit's gloves. She must have put it on while she was talking.

"How did I do *that*?" she said. The glove had been far too small. "I must be shrinking again!"

Alice returned to the table. She guessed she was about two feet high. And getting smaller. She realized that it must be the fan she was using to cool herself. Alice dropped the fan in a flash. She was just in time to save herself from shrinking away to nothing.

"That was a narrow escape!" Alice said. She was quite relieved to see that she was still there.

She ran for the garden door, but it was locked again. The golden key was back on the table.

Things are worse than ever, Alice thought. *I've never been this small before, never!*

Suddenly her foot slipped and there was a splash. She was up to her chin in salt water. At first she assumed she'd fallen into the sea. Then she realized it was the pool of tears she'd cried when she was nine feet tall.

Alice swam around, looking for a way out. "I shall be punished for crying so much," she said. "I'll be drowned in my own tears!"

Something splashed nearby. At first glance, she thought it was a walrus or a hippo. Then she realized it was only a mouse.

Everything was so strange down here. It wouldn't be strange at all if the mouse could talk. She spoke to it first. "O Mouse," she called. She thought this must be the proper way to call a mouse. "O Mouse, do you know the way out?"

The Mouse met her eyes. But he did not reply.

He must not understand English, Alice thought. Maybe he's a French mouse!

So she called, *"Où est ma chatte?"* That was the first sentence in her French book. She forgot until she said the words that it meant: "Where is my cat?"

The Mouse leaped out of the water in fright.

"I beg your pardon!" Alice cried. "I forgot you don't like cats."

"Not like cats!" the Mouse said in a shrill voice. "Would *you* like cats if you were me?"

"Maybe not," Alice said. "Please don't be angry. I wish I could show you our cat, Dinah. I think you'd like cats if you saw her. She is such a sweet, quiet little thing." Alice kept talking as she swam. "She purrs and purrs. And she's so soft. And she's just terrific at catching mice—oh, I'm sorry!" The Mouse looked especially offended. "We won't talk about Dinah, if you'd rather not."

"We, indeed!" the Mouse cried. He was trembling. "As if *I* would talk about them. Cats . . . nasty things! Don't let me hear the word again!"

"I won't," Alice promised. She tried to think of something else to talk about. "Are you . . . fond of . . . dogs?"

The Mouse started to swim away.

"Oh! I've offended him again," Alice said. She called after him, "Mouse, please come back! We won't talk about cats! Or dogs, either!"

The Mouse paddled back to her. His furry face had turned very pale. "Let's find the shore," he told her. "And then I will tell you the story of why I hate cats and dogs."

This seemed like a good idea to Alice. The pool had become very crowded with animals that had fallen in. She saw a Dodo and a Lory and many other creatures.

Together, everyone swam to the shore.

CHAPTER 3

A Caucus Race

The animals gathered on the bank of the pool of tears. But they were cranky. They were soaking wet and very uncomfortable.

They had a long talk about how to get dry. Alice found herself talking with them like she'd known them all her life. It seemed quite natural.

At last the Mouse spoke up. "Sit down, all of you! Listen. *I* know how to make you dry."

They sat in a circle with the Mouse in the middle. "Are you ready?" he called. "This is the driest thing I know." Then he began to talk about politics. He went on and on, like he was reading out loud from the most boring book.

"Ugh!" said the Lory with a shiver.

The Mouse talked on and on. It was awfully dull. After a while, he paused. He turned to Alice. "How are you, my dear?" he asked.

"As wet as ever," Alice said. She sighed. "It doesn't seem to dry me at all."

"In that case," the Dodo spoke up, "the best thing to get us dry would be a caucus race."

"What is a caucus race?" Alice asked.

"The best way to explain it is to do it," the Dodo said.

The Dodo marked off a race course. It was sort of a circle—he said the exact shape didn't matter. Then Alice and the animals were told to start running wherever they wanted on the circle. They could start whenever they wanted.

They could also stop whenever they wanted. Because of this, it was hard to know when the race was over.

After they had been running for a half hour or so, they were dry again. The Dodo called out, "The race is finished!"

The creatures crowded around. They were out of breath. "But who has won?" they asked.

"*Everybody* has won," the Dodo said after much thought. "And *all* must have prizes."

"But who will give the prizes?" the creatures asked.

"*She* will, of course," said the Dodo, as if it were obvious. He pointed at Alice.

The animals ran to her. They jumped up and down. "Prizes! Prizes!" they yelled.

Alice had no idea what to do. Finally she pulled out a box of candies from her pocket. (She was lucky that the salt water had not ruined them.) She handed out the candies as prizes.

There was exactly one piece for everyone. Except for herself.

"She must have a prize, too," said the Mouse.

"Of course," the Dodo replied. "What else do you have in your pocket?" he asked Alice.

"Only a thimble," Alice said sadly.

"Hand it over," said the Dodo.

Then they all crowded around her again. The Dodo presented the thimble to Alice as her prize. He gave a short speech, and everyone cheered.

Alice thought the whole thing very absurd. But they looked so serious, she didn't dare laugh.

Finally the animals sat in a circle again.

"You promised to tell me your story," Alice reminded the Mouse. She added in a whisper, "And why it is you hate . . . C . . . and D."

"Mine is a long and sad tale!" said the Mouse.

"It *is* a long tail," Alice said. She gazed in wonder at the Mouse's tail. "But why do you call it sad?" she asked, puzzled.

The Mouse had started his story, but Alice was still thinking of his tail.

"You're not paying attention!" the Mouse snapped. "What are you thinking about?"

"I beg your pardon," Alice said politely. "You had reached the middle, I think?"

"I had *not*!" the Mouse cried angrily.

"A knot!" Alice said. She always wanted to make herself useful. "Let me help you untie it."

The Mouse got up and walked away. "You insult me by talking such nonsense," he sniffed.

"I didn't mean it!" Alice pleaded. "Please come back and finish your story!"

But the Mouse hurried away.

"What a pity," the Lory said, and sighed.

"I wish I had our Dinah here," Alice said. "*She'd* soon fetch him back."

"And who is Dinah?" asked the Lory.

"Dinah's our cat," Alice said without thinking. "She's so good at catching mice! And you should see her go after birds! She'll eat a bird as soon as look at it!"

This caused a rush of excitement among the creatures, and they ran off, each in different directions. Alice was soon all alone.

"I wish I hadn't mentioned Dinah," she said sadly. "Nobody down here seems to like her."

Alice began to cry again. She was feeling very sorry for herself. Then she heard footsteps in the distance. She looked up. She hoped it might be the Mouse, ready to forgive her and finish his story.

CHAPTER 4

The Rabbit Sends in a Little Bill

Iₜ was the White Rabbit. He was hurrying through the hall, muttering, "The Duchess! Oh, my fur and whiskers! She'll be so angry. Where did I drop them?"

Alice realized he must be searching for his fan and white gloves. She started to look for them, too. But they were nowhere to be seen.

That's when the Rabbit noticed her. "Mary Ann!" he yelled. "What *are* you doing here? Run home and fetch me my gloves and a fan. Quickly!"

Alice was so frightened, she ran off at once.

She didn't even tell him her name was not Mary Ann.

"He thought I was his maid," she said as she ran out of the hallway. "How surprised he'll be! Still, I'd better get him his fan and gloves. *If* I can find them."

As she said this, she realized she was no longer indoors. She came upon a small road and, there, happened upon a little house. A brass plate on the door said w. RABBIT.

She rushed in and hurried upstairs.

"How strange to be running errands for a rabbit," Alice said. "I suppose I'll be running errands for Dinah next!"

Upstairs, she found a fan and a few pairs of gloves. She grabbed them and was just about to leave when she spotted a tiny bottle.

There was no label on it that said DRINK ME, but she decided to drink it, anyway.

"I know *something* interesting will happen," she

said. "I hope I'll grow large again. I am so tired of being such a tiny little thing!"

It did make her grow, and fast. She had only finished half the bottle when she felt her head against the ceiling. She quickly dropped the bottle.

"That's enough," she said. "I hope I don't grow more. As it is, I can't get out the door!"

But it was too late. She went on growing. Soon she had to kneel on the floor. In another minute, there wasn't room for her to do even that. She had to lie down with one elbow against the door. Then she had to put one arm out the window and one foot up the chimney.

Finally, she stopped growing. That was good, because there was nowhere else to go. But she was also very uncomfortable. And there was no chance of her getting out of the room now.

"Mary Ann!" she heard from outside the window. "Fetch me my gloves this minute!"

It was the White Rabbit. She trembled, forgetting she was now a thousand times bigger than him. She had no reason to be afraid.

The Rabbit tried the door, but Alice's elbow was pressed against it. He couldn't get it open.

"Then I'll go around and try the window," Alice heard him say.

You will not! Alice thought. When she heard the Rabbit under the window, she reached out a hand and grabbed at the air. She saw a small greenhouse outside and tried not to hit it, but the Rabbit must have knocked into it himself, because she heard a shriek and the crash of broken glass.

"Pat!" Alice heard the Rabbit cry. "Tell me, what's that in the window?"

Another voice—Alice assumed it was Pat's—answered. "It's an arm, Your Honor."

"It's got no business there!" the Rabbit yelled. "Take it away!"

Alice spread her fingers and grabbed at the air

again. This time, there were *two* little shrieks. And more sounds of broken glass.

She heard something being wheeled over. There were now many voices talking. "Where's the other ladder? . . . Bill's got it . . . Bill, bring it here! . . . Put them in this corner . . . No, tie them together first . . . They don't reach high enough . . . They'll do just fine . . . Bill, catch hold of this rope . . . Mind that loose shingle . . . Oh, it's coming down! Look out below!" (A loud crash.) "Bill, look what you did! . . . Who will go down the chimney? . . . Bill, of course . . . Bill, the master says you've got to go down the chimney!"

"So Bill's going down the chimney, is he?" Alice said. "They make Bill do everything!"

Alice had her foot in the fireplace. She waited until she heard scratching in the chimney, then gave a little kick.

"There goes Bill!" she heard the voices say. There was some scrambling to catch him.

The Rabbit shouted, "Burn the house down!"

Now Alice had had enough. She called as loud as she could, "If you do, I'll set Dinah on you!"

Dead silence. Alice waited to see what they'd do next. A shower of pebbles came through the window. Some hit her in the face.

But when the pebbles fell to the floor, they turned into little cakes. *If I eat one, it's sure to change my size,* she thought. *It couldn't possibly make me larger, so it must make me smaller!*

Alice swallowed a cake. She was thrilled to find herself shrinking. When she was small enough to fit through the door, she ran outside.

There she saw a crowd of animals. In the middle of the crowd, a lizard was being bandaged up by two guinea pigs. Alice wondered if the lizard was poor Bill, the animal she had kicked out of the chimney. Everyone else rushed at Alice. But she ran madly away into the woods.

"The first thing I've got to do," Alice said as she wandered the woods, "is grow to my right size. Then I need to find that lovely garden."

It was an excellent plan. The only thing was, she had no idea how to do it.

"I suppose I should eat or drink something," Alice said. "But what?"

She looked around. There were flowers and trees and grass. But there was nothing obvious to eat or drink.

There was a large mushroom growing near her. It was about her height. She looked under it and on both sides of it and behind it. Then she decided she may as well look on top of it.

She stood on tiptoe and peeked over the edge of the mushroom. Her eyes met those of a giant blue caterpillar.

CHAPTER 5

Advice from a Caterpillar

The Caterpillar gazed at Alice for quite some time in silence. At last he spoke in a slow, sleepy voice. "Who are *you*?" he asked.

"I-I hardly know, sir," Alice found herself saying. "I knew who I *was* this morning. But I think I changed several times since then."

"Explain yourself!" the Caterpillar snapped.

"I can't explain *myself,* sir," Alice said sadly. "Because I'm not myself, you see."

"I don't see," said the Caterpillar.

"Being so many different sizes in one day is very confusing," Alice said.

"It isn't," the Caterpillar said.

"Maybe you don't think so now," Alice said. "But when you turn into a butterfly one day, I think you'll feel a bit strange. Don't you?"

"Not a bit," said the Caterpillar.

"Well, maybe *you'd* feel no different," Alice said. "All I know is, it feels very strange to *me.*"

"You!" said the Caterpillar. "Who are *you*?"

Which brought them back to the beginning.

Alice was getting annoyed. "I think you should tell me who *you* are first," she said.

"Why?"

This was a puzzling question. Since Alice could not think of a good reason, and since the Caterpillar seemed so grumpy, she turned away.

"Come back," the Caterpillar said. "I have something important to say!"

This sounded promising. Alice returned to the mushroom to hear it.

"Keep your temper," the Caterpillar said.

"Is that all?" Alice said.

"No."

The Caterpillar was silent for a long while. At last he said, "What size do you want to be?"

She thought a moment. "A *little* larger," she said. "Three inches is a wretched height to be."

"It is a very good height!" the Caterpillar shouted. He stretched himself out to his full length. He was exactly three inches tall.

"But I'm not used to it!" Alice cried.

"You'll get used to it," the Caterpillar said.

Finally, he yawned and shook himself. Then he got off the mushroom and crawled away. He called out, "One side will make you grow taller. The other side will make you grow shorter."

One side of what? Alice thought. *The other side of what?*

"Of the mushroom," the Caterpillar said, as if she'd said it out loud. He crawled out of sight.

Alice looked at the mushroom. She tried to decide which side was which. The mushroom was perfectly round, so it was hard to tell.

At last, she stretched her arms around as far as they would go. She broke off a bit of the mushroom in each hand.

She nibbled a little from her right hand. The next moment she felt a hard smack under her chin. Her chin had struck her foot!

Frightened, she tried to nibble some from her left hand. Her chin was so close to her foot, there was hardly room to open her mouth. She was able to squeeze in just one bite.

She began to grow. "My head's free at last!" she cried. When she looked down, all she could see was a long length of neck. It rose like a stalk from a sea of green leaves below.

"What *can* that green stuff be?" Alice said.

"And where *have* my shoulders gone? And oh, my poor hands. How is it I can't see you?"

There seemed to be no chance of getting her hands up to her head, so she tried to get her head down to her hands.

Alice was delighted to find that her neck could bend easily in any direction, like a snake. She zigzagged her head through the trees. Finally, she found her hands.

She set to work carefully nibbling one piece of the mushroom and then the other. She grew sometimes taller and sometimes shorter. At last, she brought herself down to her usual height. With this done, she set off to find the flower garden. Suddenly she spied a house in the distance. The house was very small. She didn't want to scare whoever lived inside, so she ate another bit of the mushroom. She did not go near the house until she was nine inches tall.

CHAPTER 6

Pig and Pepper

⸙

Alice wasn't sure if she should knock on the door. Suddenly a footman ran out of the woods. (She thought of him as a footman because he was wearing a fancy uniform. If she were judging by his face, she would have thought of him as a fish.) The Fish-Footman knocked on the door. Another footman, this one with the face of a frog, opened it. They both wore powdered white wigs. Alice crept closer to the house to listen.

The Fish-Footman gave the Frog-Footman a

giant letter. "For the Duchess," he announced. "An invitation from the Queen to play croquet."

Then they bowed very low, and their wigs got stuck together. Alice laughed so hard, she had to hide deeper in the woods.

When Alice came out of the woods, the Fish-Footman was gone. The Frog-Footman was sitting by the door staring into the sky.

Alice approached the door and knocked.

"There's no use in knocking," the Frog-Footman said. "For two reasons. One, I am on the same side of the door as you are. And two, because they are making so much noise inside, no one could hear you."

There *was* a lot of noise inside the house. Alice heard howls and sneezes and, every now and then, a great crash.

"I shall sit here," the Frog-Footman said, "until tomorrow—"

At this point, the door opened. A large plate

came flying out, straight at the Frog-Footman's head. It grazed his nose and shattered on the ground.

"—or the next day maybe," the Frog-Footman continued, as if nothing had happened.

Alice decided to go inside, anyway. She stepped into a large kitchen. The Duchess was sitting on a stool, holding a crying baby. The cook was leaning over the fire, stirring soup. The room was filled with the smell of the soup.

Alice sneezed. "There's too much pepper in that soup!" she cried.

There was also too much pepper in the *air*. The Duchess sneezed. Even the baby stopped crying to sneeze. The only two creatures in the room who did *not* sneeze were the cook and a large cat. The cat sat on the ground, grinning from ear to ear.

"Please, would you tell me," Alice began, not wanting to be rude, "why does your cat grin like that?"

"It's a Cheshire-Cat," the Duchess said. "That's why. Pig!"

Alice jumped, thinking the Duchess was talking about her. But it seemed that she was talking to the baby.

Alice continued, "I didn't know Cheshire-Cats grinned. I didn't know cats *could* grin."

"You don't know very much," said the Duchess.

The cook took the soup off the fire. Then she began throwing everything nearby at the Duchess and the baby. It was a shower of pots, pans, and dishes. The Duchess took no notice. The baby howled. Since it had been howling before, Alice wasn't sure if the dishes were hurting it or not.

"*Please* mind what you're doing!" Alice cried, jumping out of the way. A saucer sailed by the baby's face. "Oh, his poor nose!"

"Here," the Duchess said. "You hold it if you want." She pushed the baby into Alice's arms. "I must go get ready to play croquet with the Queen," the Duchess added. She hurried out of the room. The cook threw a frying pan after her.

The baby squirmed wildly in Alice's arms. She could barely keep a hold of it.

She ran out of the house with the baby. *I have to take this baby away with me,* she thought. *It's far too dangerous in there.*

The little thing grunted in her arms.

"Don't grunt!" she scolded. She pushed the blankets aside so she could see the baby's face.

The baby had an odd nose. It looked more like a snout than a nose. Also, its eyes were terribly small. It wasn't a very cute baby.

The baby grunted again. Alice assumed it was probably just crying. But it couldn't be crying—there were no tears.

"If you're going to turn into a pig, my dear," Alice said in all seriousness, "I'll have nothing more to do with you."

The little thing grunted again loudly. Alice looked into its face in alarm. This time there could be no mistake: It *was* a pig. It seemed quite absurd for her to carry it any longer, so she set the pig down on the ground. It trotted happily away into the woods.

"It was a dreadfully ugly baby," Alice said. "But it makes a rather handsome pig."

Alice was startled to see the Cheshire-Cat sitting on the branch of a tree. The cat grinned at her. It looked nice enough. Still, it had very long claws and many teeth, so she felt it should be treated with respect.

"Cheshire-Cat," she called up politely. "Would you tell me please which way to go from here?"

"That depends on where you want to get," the Cheshire-Cat said.

"I don't care where——" Alice said.

"Then it doesn't matter which way you go," the Cheshire-Cat answered.

"——so long as I get *somewhere*," Alice added.

"You're sure to do that if you walk long enough."

Alice tried another question. "What kind of people live around here?"

"In *that* direction," said the Cheshire-Cat, waving its right paw, "lives a Hatter. And in *that* direction"—it pointed the other paw—"lives a March Hare. Visit either. They're both mad."

"But I don't want to be around mad people," Alice said.

"You can't help that. We're all mad here. I'm mad. You're mad."

"How do you know I'm mad?" Alice asked.

"You must be," said the Cheshire-Cat. "Or you wouldn't have come here."

Alice didn't think that proved anything.

"Will you be playing croquet with the Queen today?" the Cheshire-Cat asked.

"I would like to very much," Alice said. "But I haven't been invited yet."

"You'll see me there," the Cheshire-Cat said. Then it vanished.

Alice wasn't surprised. She was quite used to odd things happening by now.

The Cheshire-Cat appeared again.

"By the way, what became of the baby?" it said. "I nearly forgot to ask."

"It turned into a pig," Alice said.

"I thought it would," the Cat replied. It began to vanish again, but this time quite slowly, beginning with the tail and ending with the grin. The grin remained some time after the rest of the Cat had gone.

"I've seen a cat without a grin," Alice said, "but a grin without a cat! That's the most curious thing I've ever seen in my life!"

Alice waited to see if the Cat would reappear. When it didn't, she walked toward the March Hare's house.

"I've seen hatters before," she said to herself. "The March Hare will be more interesting. Besides, it's May. Maybe he won't be *raving*."

CHAPTER 7

A Mad Tea-Party

When Alice reached the March Hare's house, she found a tea table set out in front. The March Hare and the Mad Hatter were having tea together. In the chair between them was a Dormouse. He was fast asleep, and they were resting their elbows on him and talking over his head.

The table was far too large for just three. Teacups and plates were set up at every place. Even so, the March Hare, the Mad Hatter, and the Dormouse were crammed together at one corner of the table. "No room! No room!" they cried when they saw Alice coming.

"There's *plenty* of room!" Alice said. She sat down in a large armchair at one end of the table.

"Have some lemonade," the March Hare said.

Alice looked around the table. All she saw was tea. "I don't see any lemonade," she said.

"There isn't any," said the March Hare.

"Then that wasn't very polite of you to offer it," Alice said angrily.

"It wasn't very polite of you to sit down without being invited," said the March Hare.

"Your hair wants cutting," the Hatter added.

"You shouldn't make personal remarks," Alice said. "It's rude."

The Hatter opened his eyes very wide when she said this. But what he said to Alice was, "What day of the month is it?"

He had taken out his pocket watch. He shook it and held it to his ear.

Alice tried to recall. "It's the fourth," she said.

"My watch is two days wrong!" sighed the Hatter. "I told you butter wouldn't be good for it!" He looked angrily at the March Hare.

"It was the *best* butter," the March Hare said.

"Yes, but some crumbs must have gotten in as well," the Hatter grumbled. "You shouldn't have put it in with the bread knife."

The March Hare took hold of the watch. Then he dipped it into his cup of tea.

Alice watched with some curiosity. "What a funny watch!" she said. "It tells the day of the month, but it doesn't tell what o'clock it is!"

"Why should it?" the Hatter said. "Does *your* watch tell you what year it is?"

"Of course not," said Alice. "But that's because it stays the same year for a long time."

"Just like mine," the Hatter said.

Alice was puzzled. "I don't quite understand," she said as politely as she could.

"The Dormouse is still asleep," said the Hatter. He poured a little hot tea on his nose.

The Dormouse shook his head. Without opening his eyes, he mumbled, "Of course. Just what I was going to say myself."

The March Hare yawned. "I vote the young lady tell us a story."

Alice was alarmed. "I'm afraid I don't know one," she said.

"Then the Dormouse will!" the March Hare and the Mad Hatter cried together. They pinched the Dormouse on both sides.

The Dormouse slowly opened his eyes. "I wasn't asleep," he said softly.

"Tell us a story!" the March Hare demanded.

"Yes, please do!" Alice found herself saying.

"And be quick about it," the Hatter added. "Or you'll be asleep again before it's done."

"Once upon a time there were three little sisters," the Dormouse began quickly. "Their names were Elsie, Lacie, and Tillie, and they lived at the bottom of a well, and—"

"What did they live on?" Alice asked. She was always interested in questions of eating and drinking.

"They lived on treacle," the Dormouse said.

Alice was quite sure that treacle was sticky-sweet molasses. "They couldn't have lived on just that, you know," she said. "They would have been ill."

"So they were," said the Dormouse. "*Very* ill."

"But why did they live at the bottom of a well?" she asked.

"Have some more tea," the March Hare said.

"I haven't had any yet," Alice said. "So I can't take any more."

"You mean you can't take less," the Hatter said. "It's easy to take more than nothing."

Alice didn't know what to say to this, so she helped herself to some tea. Then she asked the

Dormouse again, "Why did they live at the bottom of a well?"

The Dormouse took a minute or two to think about it. Then he said, "It was a treacle well."

"There's no such thing!" Alice burst out.

"Shhh!" said the Hatter and the March Hare.

"If you can't be polite, finish the story yourself," the Dormouse said. He started to sulk.

"No, please go on!" Alice said. "I won't interrupt again, I promise."

"And so," the Dormouse continued, "the three sisters were learning to draw—"

"What did they draw?" Alice asked. She had already forgotten her promise.

"Treacle," the Dormouse said.

"I want a clean cup," the Hatter announced. "Let's all move one place on."

He moved to another chair. The Dormouse followed, moving into the Hatter's chair. The March Hare moved into the Dormouse's chair.

Alice unwillingly took the chair of the March Hare. The Hatter was the only one who gained anything from the change. Alice was a good deal worse off than before—since the March Hare had just knocked the milk jug onto his plate.

"They were learning to draw," the Dormouse said, continuing the story. Then he yawned. He spoke again, slowly, "And they drew all sorts of things . . . everything that begins with M."

"Why M?" Alice asked.

"Why not?" said the March Hare.

Alice kept quiet.

The Dormouse had closed his eyes. The Hatter pinched him, and he woke with a little shriek. He went on drowsily, ". . . that begins with M, such as mousetraps, and the moon, and muchness. Did you ever see such a thing as a drawing of muchness? And . . ."

"If you ask me, I don't think—" Alice started.

"Then you shouldn't talk," the Hatter said.

His rudeness was more than Alice could bear. She stormed off in disgust. She walked as far away as she could from the tea table, but they didn't call after her. They didn't seem to care that she had gone.

She looked back and saw that the Hatter and the March Hare were trying to stuff the sleeping Dormouse into the teapot.

"That was the worst tea party I've ever been to in my whole life!" Alice cried.

As she said this, she noticed that one of the trees nearby had a door leading into it. Without another thought, she stepped inside.

Once again, she found herself in the little hallway with the little door and the little key on top of the little table. She quickly unlocked the door and nibbled some of the mushroom she kept in her pocket until she was the perfect size to fit through it.

Then, at long last, she went into the garden.

CHAPTER 8

The Queen's Croquet-Ground

$\backsim$

A large rose tree stood at the entrance to the garden. The roses growing on it were white. Three gardeners (who looked like playing cards) were busy painting them red.

Curious, Alice approached. "Why are you painting these roses?" she asked.

Two of the cards said nothing. But the third card said in a low voice, "You see, miss, this should have been a *red* rose tree. But we put a white one in by mistake. If the Queen finds it, we will lose our heads, you know——"

At this moment, the card next to him cried, "The Queen!" The three gardeners threw themselves on the ground, hiding their faces.

Alice heard the sound of marching. She turned, excited to see the Queen.

First came the soldiers wearing clubs. Next came the courtiers wearing diamonds. Then came the royal children, all wearing hearts. The guests came next. There were mostly kings and queens, and Alice recognized the White Rabbit. He hurried by nervously, not noticing her. Then came the Knave of Hearts, carrying the King's crown on a velvet cushion. And last of all came the King and Queen of Hearts.

When the Queen saw Alice, she stopped. "Who is this?" she asked the Knave of Hearts. He just bowed and smiled in reply.

"Idiot!" the Queen shrieked. She turned to Alice. "What is your name, child?"

"My name is Alice, Your Majesty."

"And who are *they*?" the Queen asked. She pointed to the three gardeners. They were still lying flat on the ground. Since they were lying on their faces, the pattern on their backs was the same as that of the rest of the pack. The Queen could not tell if they were gardeners, soldiers, or three of her own children.

"How should *I* know?" Alice said. She was surprised at her own courage.

The Queen turned crimson with fury. "Off with her head!" she screamed.

"Nonsense," Alice said.

The Queen's eyes blazed.

Timidly, the King said to the Queen, "My dear, she is only a child."

The Queen turned away angrily. She ordered the three gardeners up. "Off with their heads!" she shouted.

The Queen and King moved on. When they were gone, Alice hid the gardeners in a large flowerpot.

"Are their heads off?" the Queen shouted behind her.

Her soldiers were confused when they couldn't find the gardeners. But to the Queen, they replied, "Their heads are gone, Your Majesty!"

"That's right!" the Queen shouted. "Can you play croquet?"

The soldiers didn't answer. Instead, they looked to Alice. Clearly the question was meant for her.

"Yes!" shouted Alice.

"Come on, then!" roared the Queen.

So Alice walked with the rest of the royal guests toward the croquet field.

The White Rabbit came up beside her. "It's a very fine day!" he said in high, nervous voice.

"Very," Alice said. "Where's the Duchess?"

"Hush!" the Rabbit said. Into her ear he whispered, "The Queen put her in prison."

"Get to your places!" the Queen commanded.

The guests ran in all directions. Soon the game began. It was the most curious croquet game Alice had ever seen. The croquet balls were hedgehogs. The mallets were live flamingos. The soldiers had to stand on their hands and feet to make the arches.

Alice found the game rather difficult, mainly because she had a hard time controlling her flamingo. Every time she got it into position, it twisted its neck and looked up at her with the oddest expression. She couldn't help but laugh. Plus, her hedgehog kept crawling away. And the soldiers were always walking around to different spots, so the arches were never in the same place.

The players all played at the same time. They fought over hedgehogs. Soon, the Queen was stomping around. She was screaming, "Off with his head!" or, "Off with her head!"

Alice began to feel uneasy. *What will become of me?* she thought. *They're dreadfully fond of getting rid of people's heads here. It's a wonder anyone here has a head!*

She was looking for a way to escape when she noticed a curious shape in the air.

It looked like a grin. A grin without a head attached.

"Why, it's the Cheshire-Cat!" she said excitedly. "Now I'll have someone to talk to!"

"How are you getting on?" asked the Cat as soon as he had enough of a mouth to speak with.

"I don't think they play at all fairly," Alice complained when the Cat's ears appeared.

"How do you like the Queen?" the Cat asked.

"Not at all," Alice said. "She so extremely—"

Just then, she noticed that the Queen was right

behind her, listening. "——likely to win. It's hardly worth finishing the game," Alice said.

The Queen smiled and walked on.

"Who are you talking to?" the King asked Alice. He was standing beside her. He gazed at the Cheshire-Cat with great curiosity.

"A friend of mine," Alice said. "A Cheshire-Cat. Allow me to introduce you."

"I'd rather not," the Cheshire-Cat said.

"Don't be rude!" the King snapped. "This cat must be removed." He called to the Queen. "My dear! I wish you would have this cat removed!"

The Queen had only one way to do that.

"Off with its head!" she shouted without even looking over.

But when the soldier arrived, there was an argument. Everyone turned to Alice to settle it.

The soldier said that you couldn't remove a head unless there was a body to remove it from. The King said that anything with a head could be beheaded. The Queen said that if something wasn't done about it soon, she'd remove everyone's head.

The crowd looked very nervous.

Alice could think of nothing to say except, "The cat belongs to the Duchess. You'd better ask *her* about it."

"But she's in prison," the Queen said.

The Cheshire-Cat's head began to fade away. Soon, the cat had vanished completely. The King and the soldiers ran around looking for it. But everyone else just shrugged and went back to playing croquet.

CHAPTER 9

Who Stole the Tarts?

❦

Not much later there was a cry in the distance. "The trial is starting!" Alice heard. *What trial?* she thought. She followed the crowd, curious.

Alice found the King and Queen seated on their thrones. A crowd of little birds and beasts, as well as the whole pack of cards, was in the courtroom. The Knave of Hearts was standing before them in chains. Soldiers guarded him. The White Rabbit stood near the King. He had a trumpet in one hand and a scroll of parchment in the other.

In the very middle of the court was a table with a huge tray of tarts on it. They looked delicious.

Alice had never been in a courtroom before. But she had read about them in books. She knew that there would be a judge. (For this trial, the judge was the King himself. Alice knew because he was wearing a powdered white wig.) She also knew that there would be a jury box. And in this trial, the jury box was filled with twelve little creatures—a mix of different animals.

The jurors had slates on which to write down different pieces of evidence. Some of the jurors were already writing, although there was nothing to important to remember.

One juror—Bill the Lizard—had a pencil that squeaked. This, of course, Alice could *not* stand. She crept behind him and snatched the pencil away. She did it so quickly that poor Bill had no idea what happened to it and was left to write with one finger for the rest of the day, which was of very little use because it left no mark on his slate.

"Silence in the court!" the White Rabbit called.

"Read the charges!" the King yelled.

The White Rabbit blew three blasts on his trumpet. Then he unrolled the parchment scroll and began to read:

The Queen of Hearts, she made some tarts,

All on a summer day;

The Knave of Hearts, he stole those tarts,

And took them quite away!

"Consider your verdict," the King told the jury.

"Not yet," the Rabbit interrupted. "There's a great deal to come before that."

"Call the first witness, then," said the King.

This was the Hatter. He came in with a teacup

in one hand and a piece of bread and butter in the other. "I beg your pardon, Your Majesty, for bringing these in," he said. "But I hadn't quite finished my tea when I was sent for."

"You should have finished," the King said. "When did you begin?"

The Hatter looked at the March Hare, who had followed him into court with the Dormouse. "Fourteenth of March, I think," said the Hatter.

"Fifteenth," said the March Hare.

"Sixteenth," said the Dormouse.

"Write that down," the King told the jury. The jury eagerly wrote down all three dates. Then they added them up and divided them into nonsense.

"Take off your hat," the King told the Hatter.

"It isn't mine," said the Hatter.

"Stolen!" the King yelled.

The jury wrote this down.

"I keep them to sell," the Hatter explained. "I have no hats of my own. I am a hatter."

"Give your evidence," the King said. "And don't be nervous, or I'll have your head removed on the spot."

This made the Hatter even more nervous. He looked anxiously at the Queen. She stared back angrily. Nervously, the Hatter bit a large piece out of his teacup instead of his bread and butter.

At this moment, Alice felt a curious thing. It seemed like she was growing larger. At first she thought she should get up and leave the court. But on second thought, she decided to stay where she was as long as there was room for her.

"I wish you wouldn't squeeze so," said the Dormouse. He was sitting next to her. "I can hardly breathe."

"I can't help it," Alice said. "I'm growing."

"You have no right to grow *here*," the Dormouse snapped.

"Don't talk nonsense," Alice said. "You know you're growing, too."

"Yes, but I grow at a normal pace. Not in a ridiculous fashion," the Dormouse said. He got up and moved to another seat.

The Hatter was still trying to give his evidence. "Then the Dormouse said—" the Hatter was saying. He glanced over at the Dormouse. He was fast asleep.

"After that," the Hatter continued, "I cut some more bread and butter—"

"But what did the Dormouse say?" a creature from the jury asked.

"That, I can't remember," the Hatter said.

"You *must* remember," the King said. "Or I'll have your head removed."

The Hatter dropped his teacup. He went down on one knee. He was shaking. "I'm a poor man, Your Majesty," he pleaded.

"You're a *very* poor *speaker*," the King said. "If that's all you have to say, you may stand down."

"I can't go any lower," the Hatter protested. "I'm on the floor now as it is."

"Then you may *sit* down," the King said.

The Hatter rushed out of the court without another word.

"Just take off his head outside," the Queen told one of the soldiers. But the Hatter was out of sight before the soldier could reach him.

"Call the next witness!" the King yelled.

The next witness was the Duchess's cook. She was carrying the pepper with her. Everyone sneezed as she entered the court.

"Give your evidence," the King said.

"Won't," the cook replied.

The King crossed his arms. He frowned at the cook. "What are tarts made of?" he asked her.

"Pepper, mostly," the cook said at once.

"Treacle," said a sleepy voice nearby.

"Remove the Dormouse's head!" the Queen

shrieked in excitement. "Turn the Dormouse out of court! Pinch him! Off with his whiskers!"

For some minutes, the whole court was in confusion. By the time they made the Dormouse leave, the cook had disappeared.

"Nevermind!" the King said. "Call the next witness."

Alice watched the White Rabbit as he fumbled over the list. She was very curious to see who the next witness would be. And she was *very* surprised when the White Rabbit read out in a loud, shrill voice the name "Alice!"

CHAPTER 10

Alice's Evidence

∽

"Here!" Alice cried. She had forgotten how large she had grown. When she jumped up, she knocked over the jury box. The creatures on the jury fell out onto their heads.

"Oh, I *beg* your pardon!" Alice exclaimed. She picked them up as quickly as she could. When all the jurors were back in their box, Alice approached the witness stand.

"What do you know about this?" the King asked.

"Nothing," Alice said.

"Nothing *at all*?" the King persisted.

"Nothing at all," Alice said.

"That's very important," the King said, turning to the jury. They wrote it down.

The White Rabbit spoke up. "*Un*important, Your Majesty means, of course," he said.

"*Un*important, of course," the King said. "That's what I meant. Important. Unimportant. Important. Unimportant. Important—" He went on, as if trying to see which word he liked best.

Some creatures in the jury wrote down one word. Some wrote down the other. Alice could see this. *But it doesn't matter a bit,* she thought.

The King called out, "Silence!" He read aloud from his book: "Rule forty-two. All persons more than a mile high must leave the court."

Everybody looked to Alice.

"*I'm* not a mile high," she protested.

"You are," the King said.

"I won't go," Alice said. "Besides, that's not a real rule. You just made it up."

"It's the oldest rule in the book," the King said.

"Then it would be rule number one," Alice said.

The King turned very pale. He shut his book. "Consider your verdict," he told the jury.

The White Rabbit jumped up, waving a piece of paper. "There's more evidence, Your Majesty," he announced. "A letter written by the prisoner, the Knave of Hearts, to . . . somebody."

"It must have been *to* somebody," the King said. "Unless it was written to nobody."

The White Rabbit opened the envelope. "It's not a letter at all, Your Majesty. It's a poem."

"Please, Your Majesty," the Knave of Hearts called out. "I didn't write it. They can't prove that I did. There's no name signed at the end."

The King thought for a moment. "If you didn't sign it, that only makes it worse. You would have signed your name like an honest man unless you wanted to make some mischief."

The crowd applauded. It was the first clever thing the King had said all day.

"That proves his guilt, of course," the Queen said. "So off with his—"

"It doesn't prove anything of the sort!" Alice interrupted. She had grown so large that she wasn't afraid to speak out at all.

"Hold your tongue!" the Queen shouted.

"I won't," Alice said.

"Off with her head!" the Queen screamed at the top of her lungs.

Nobody moved.

"Who cares for you?" Alice said. She had grown to her full height by now. "You're nothing but a pack of cards!"

At this, the whole pack of cards rose up into the air. They flew straight at Alice. She screamed. She tried to beat them off . . .

. . . and found herself lying on the riverbank. She had her head in her sister's lap. Her sister was gently brushing away some leaves that had fallen from the tree above onto her face.

"Wake up, Alice dear!" her sister was saying.

Alice opened her eyes.

"Oh, I had such a curious dream," she said. And she told her sister every single thing she could remember. She'd had the most wonderful adventures. But they had seemed so real. It was so very hard to believe it had only been a dream.

Through the Looking-Glass

CHAPTER 1

The Looking-Glass House

಄

Alice's cat Dinah had two kittens. One, the fuzzy black one, was quite the troublemaker. Alice took it aside to scold it, but it wouldn't pay any attention. She held it up to the closest looking-glass—the big mirror in the drawing room. She wanted it to see how naughty it was being.

"Look how grumpy you are," Alice told the kitten. "If you're not good, I'll put you through this looking-glass into the looking-glass house on the other side. How would you like *that*?"

Talking about the looking-glass house got Alice thinking. "I'll tell you all about the looking-glass house, kitty," she said. "First, there's the room you can see through the glass. It's the same as our drawing room, except that things go the other way. The books are something like our books, except the words go the wrong way. I know that because I've held one of our books to the mirror.

"How would you like to live in the looking-glass house, kitty? You can see a peep of the hallway now, since the door to our drawing room is open. It looks a lot like our hallway. But, you know, the area we can't see might be quite different. Oh, kitty! Let's pretend there's a way in. Let's pretend the glass is soft, so we can get through. Why, it's turning into a sort of mist now! It'll be easy enough to get through—"

As Alice said this, she climbed up on a chair right next to the mirror. She couldn't remember how she'd gotten there, but it was very strange. Certainly the glass *was* melting away, just like bright silvery mist.

In another moment Alice was through the glass. She jumped down into the looking-glass room.

What could be seen from the old room was quite boring. But everything else was as different as could be. The pictures on the wall that couldn't be seen from the old room seemed to be alive. And the clock that stood against the mirror had the face of a little old man. It grinned at her!

Alice noticed that some chess pieces had fallen on the floor. She got on her knees to pick them up. When she got closer, she saw that they were walking around and talking like little people.

"Here are the Red King and the Red Queen,"

Alice said to herself in a whisper. (She didn't want to scare them.) "And there are the White King and the White Queen sitting together near the fireplace."

Alice heard the sound of squeaking on the table behind her. She turned her head just in time to see a white pawn roll over and start kicking.

"My child! My precious Lily!" the White Queen cried. She rushed past the King, accidentally knocking him over. The King fell into the fireplace and got covered in ashes.

Alice wanted to be helpful. Since poor little Lily was screaming, she picked up the Queen and set her on the table beside her baby.

The Queen gasped. The speedy journey through the air had taken her breath away. "Mind the volcano!" she called down to the King. She pointed at the fireplace. "It blew me up here. Be careful to come up the normal way."

The King nodded. Alice watched him slowly climb up the table. It was taking him forever.

"It'll take you hours and hours to get up there!" she said. "I'd better help you, shouldn't I?" The King didn't seem to notice her question. Clearly, he couldn't hear or see her.

So Alice picked him up gently. She carried him to the table. Then, since he was covered in ashes, she dusted him off.

The King made a terrible face. He seemed very confused about what was happening to him.

"Don't make faces!" Alice cried, even though she knew the King couldn't hear. "You're making me laugh so much, I might drop you!"

Finally, she set the King down beside his Queen. "The horror!" the King said to the Queen. "I will never forget!"

Alice noticed a book on the table. She turned the pages to find some part she could read. "It's all in a language I don't know," she said.

It looked like this:

> 'Twas brillig, and the slithy toves
> Did gyre and gimble in the wabe:
> All mimsy were the borogoves,
> And the mome raths outgrabe.

She puzzled over this for some time. Then she remembered it was a looking-glass book! She held it up to the mirror, and the words went the right way again.

This is the poem that Alice read:

JABBERWOCKY

'Twas brillig, and the slithy toves
Did gyre and gimble in the wabe:
All mimsy were the borogoves,
And the mome raths outgrabe.

Beware the Jabberwock, my son!
The jaws that bite, the claws that catch!

Beware the Jubjub bird, and shun
The frumious Bandersnatch!

He took his vorpal sword in hand:
Long time the manxome foe he sought—
So rested he by the Tumtum tree,
And stood awhile in thought.

And, as in uffish thought he stood,
The Jabberwock, with eyes of flame,
Came whiffling through the tulgey wood,
And burbled as it came!

One, two! One, two! And through and through
The vorpal blade went snicker-snack!
He left it dead, and with its head
He went galumphing back.

And, has thou slain the Jabberwock?
Come to my arms, my beamish boy!
O frabjous day! Callooh! Callay!
He chortled in his joy.

'Twas brillig, and the slithy toves

Did gyre and gimble in the wabe;

All mimsy were the borogoves,

And the mome raths outgrabe.

"It seems very pretty," Alice said. "But it is *very* hard to understand!" (Alice didn't want to confess, even to herself, that she couldn't make sense of it at all.)

"But, oh!" Alice gasped, jumping up. "I have to see what the rest of the looking-glass house is like! Let's have a look at the garden first!"

She ran out of the room and down the stairs. Except, she wasn't really running. Instead, she was floating. In the looking-glass house, running was more like floating, she guessed. She floated down the stairs and through the halls. She had to stop herself at the doorway, since she was getting dizzy. She was rather glad to be able to walk normally out the door and into the garden.

CHAPTER 2

The Garden of Live Flowers

❧

"I could see the garden much better if I could just get to the top of that hill," Alice said to herself. That seemed easy enough. The only problem was that every path she took only brought her right back to the house.

She turned her back on the house and set off down the path. She would just keep going straight until she reached the hill. Then the path gave a sudden twist and she was walking into the house again.

There was nothing to do but start again.

This time, she came upon a bed of flowers.

"O Tiger Lily," Alice said, talking to a tall flower nearby. "I *wish* you could talk!"

"We *can* talk," the Tiger Lily said. "When there's someone worth talking to."

Alice was shocked. "Can *all* the flowers talk?" she whispered.

"As well as you can," the Tiger Lily said. "And a great deal louder."

"It's not good manners for us to speak first, you know," the Rose said. "Besides, I was wondering when *you* would speak. I saw you and thought your face has got *some* sense to it . . . though it doesn't look very clever. Still, you're the right color. And that goes a long way."

"I don't care about the color," the Tiger Lily said. "If only her petals curled up a little more, then she'd be all right."

Alice didn't like being criticized, so she asked,

"How can you talk so well? I've been in many gardens, but none of the flowers could talk."

"Put your hand down and feel the ground," the Tiger Lily said. "Then you'll know why."

Alice felt the ground. "It's very hard," she said. "But what does that have to do with it?"

"In most gardens, they make the beds too soft," the Tiger Lily explained. "So the flowers are always asleep."

"I never thought of that before!" Alice said.

"It is *my* opinion that you never think *at all*," the Rose said.

"I never saw anybody who looked more stupid," the Violet said.

Alice jumped—it hadn't spoken before.

"Hold your tongue!" the Tiger Lily snapped at the Violet.

Alice ignored the insults. "Are there any other people in the garden besides me?" she asked.

"There's one other flower that can move around like you," the Rose said.

"Is she like me?" Alice asked eagerly. *There's another little girl in the garden!* she thought.

"Well," the Rose said, "she has the same awkward shape as you. But she's redder. She's one of the thorny kind."

"Where does she wear her thorns?" Alice asked. She was very curious.

"Around her head, of course!" the Rose said.

"She's coming!" cried a Daisy. "I hear her!"

Alice looked around excitedly. She discovered that it was the Red Queen. "She's grown a good deal!" she said. It was true. When Alice had first seen the Red Queen with the other chess pieces, she was three inches high. Now she was half a head taller than Alice herself.

"It's the fresh air that does it," the Rose said.

"I think I'll go and meet her," Alice said.

"You can't do that," the Rose said. "My advice is that you walk the other way."

That sounded like nonsense to Alice. She set off at once for the Red Queen. To her surprise, she lost sight of her in a moment. She found herself at the door to the house again.

Alice was confused, and now quite annoyed. She looked back toward the Red Queen. She was so very far away. To reach her, Alice decided to try walking in the opposite direction.

This worked perfectly. Alice soon found herself face-to-face with the Red Queen. She could also see the hill she'd been trying to reach.

"Where do you come from?" the Red Queen asked Alice. "And where are you going? Look up, speak nicely, and curtsy while you're thinking what to say. It saves time."

Alice found herself quite nervous to be so close to a queen. "I only wanted to see what the garden was like, Your Majesty," she said.

She looked around. There were a number of tiny streams running straight across from side to side. And the ground between them was divided into little squares by short green hedges.

"It's just like a chessboard!" Alice cried. She saw some men on the squares. "It's a huge game of chess! What fun! How I *wish* I could play. I wouldn't mind being a pawn. Though of course I would *like* to be a queen best."

She glanced shyly at the real queen.

The Red Queen smiled. "That's easily arranged," she said. "You can be the White Queen's pawn. Lily's too young to play. You're in the Second Square to start. When you reach the Eighth Square, you'll be a queen."

Suddenly, the Queen grabbed Alice's hand. She started running and pulled Alice along with her. "Faster!" cried the Queen. It was strange, but the trees never changed their places as they ran past. However fast they went, they never seemed to pass anything. *I wonder if all the things are running with us?* Alice thought, puzzled.

At last, just as Alice was getting quite exhausted, they stopped. She found herself sitting on the ground, out of breath.

Alice looked around in surprise. "I think we've been under this tree the whole time!" she said. "Everything looks the same."

"Why wouldn't it?" the Queen asked.

"Well, where *I* live," Alice said, still panting a little, "you'd generally get to somewhere else if you ran very fast for a long time."

"How slow!" the Queen said. "*Here,* it takes all the running you can do to stay in place."

"I am so hot and thirsty," Alice said.

"I know what you'd like!" the Queen said. "A cookie!" She held one out.

What Alice wanted was something to drink. But she thought it might be rude to refuse. So she took the cookie and ate it. But it was very, *very* dry.

"Thirst quenched, I hope?" the Queen asked.

Alice did not know what to say to this.

"I shall leave now," the Queen said. She got up. Then she turned and said, "A pawn goes two squares on the first move, you know. You'll go quickly through the Third Square—by train, I imagine—and find the Fourth Square in no time. That square belongs to Tweedledum and Tweedledee, although you will have to pass through the woods where things have no names first. You won't remember the Fifth Square. The Sixth Square belongs to Humpty Dumpty. The Seventh Square is all forest, but a knight will show you the way. And in the Eighth Square we shall be queens together. Then it's all feasting and fun!"

At that, the Red Queen was gone.

Then Alice remembered she was a pawn now. Soon it would be time for her to move.

CHAPTER 3

Looking-Glass Insects

༄

"Tickets, please!" the train conductor called out. Alice was taking a train to the Fourth Square.

Everyone in the train compartment held a ticket—except for Alice.

"Show your ticket, child!" the conductor said.

"I haven't got a ticket," Alice said. "There wasn't a ticket office where I came from."

The conductor looked at her sternly. First he used a telescope. Then a microscope. Then an opera glass. At last he said, "You're traveling the wrong way," and left her alone.

The man sitting across from Alice was dressed in white paper. He had a white paper hat, a white paper suit, and white paper shoes. "A child so young should know which way she's going," he said. "Even if she doesn't know her own name!"

Next to the man was a goat. The goat said, "She should know the way to the ticket office. Even if she doesn't know the alphabet."

There was a beetle sitting next to the goat. (It was a very strange train, holding a great many very strange passengers.) The beetle said, "She'll have to go back from here as luggage."

"Change engines," a hoarse voice said. It was a horse.

An extremely small voice close to her ear said, "You might want to make a joke about that. Something about *horse* and *hoarse*."

Confused, Alice ignored the voice.

The man dressed in paper leaned forward. "Nevermind what they say," he told her. "Just take a return ticket every time the train stops."

"You might want to make a joke about that," the little voice close to her ear said. "Something about 'you would if you could,' you know."

Alice looked around wildly. She couldn't figure out where the voice was coming from.

"If you want a joke so badly, maybe you should make one yourself," she said.

The little voice sighed.

"You are a friend," the little voice said. "I know you won't hurt me. Even if I am an insect."

"What kind of insect?" Alice asked anxiously. What she really wanted to know was if it could sting. But she didn't think that was polite to ask.

The little voice began to answer. Then it was drowned out by the train engine.

The horse put his head out the window to see what was going on. "Don't worry," he said. "It's only a brook we have to jump over." This meant they would soon be in the Fourth Square.

Indeed, the train melted away and Alice found herself back in the woods. She was sitting under a tree with the gnat. (This was the insect she had been talking to.) It was a *very* large gnat, the size of a chicken. Still, she didn't feel nervous, since they had been talking to each other for so long.

The gnat showed Alice all the different sorts of insects that lived on this side of the looking-glass. They were sort of like insects Alice knew at home, but not exactly.

Where Alice lived, there was the horsefly. Here, there was the rocking-horse-fly. It was made entirely of wood and got around by swinging itself from branch to branch.

Where Alice lived, there was the dragonfly. Here, there was the snap-dragon-fly. Its body was made of plum pudding, its wings were holly leaves, and its head was a raisin.

Where Alice lived, there was the butterfly.

Here, there was the bread-and-butter-fly. Its wings were thin slices of bread and butter. Its body was the crust. Its head was a lump of sugar.

The gnat told Alice all this. Then it hummed around Alice's head and said, "I suppose you don't want to lose your name?"

"No, indeed!" Alice said, now worried.

"But think how easy it would be to go home without it. For instance, if your teacher wanted to call on you in class, she would say, 'Come here . . .' And then she'd stop talking, because there wouldn't be a name for her to call you. So of course you wouldn't have to go, you know."

"I'm not sure about that," Alice said. "If my teacher forgot my name, she would just call me 'Miss.' I would still have to go to class."

"Well, if she said 'Miss' and nothing more, of course you'd miss class," the gnat said. "That's a joke," it added. "I wish *you* had made it."

"Why?" Alice said. "It's a bad joke."

The gnat sighed deeply.

"You shouldn't make jokes if it makes you so unhappy," Alice said.

The gnat sighed again. It must have sighed itself away, because suddenly it was quite gone.

Alice started walking. She reached the woods where things have no names. "I wonder what will become of my name when I go in," she said. "I don't want to lose it. I know my new name would be an ugly one."

She went on talking to herself as she walked through the woods. "It's a great comfort, after being so hot, to get into the—*what*?" She stopped. She couldn't think of the word. "What *does* it call itself, I wonder? I do believe it's got no name!"

Alice was very confused. "It really *has* happened!" she said. "Who am I?"

A fawn came wandering by. It stared at her with big eyes and let her stroke its head.

"What do you call yourself?" the fawn asked.

"I wish I knew!" Alice said sadly. "What do *you* call yourself?"

"I'll tell you, if you come a little farther," the fawn said. "I can't remember here."

So they walked together through the woods. Alice put her arm around the fawn's neck like they were old friends.

But when they came out of the woods, the fawn jumped in alarm. "I'm a fawn!" it cried. "And *you*! You're a human child!" It ran away.

Alice wanted to cry. But she did remember her name now, which was *some* comfort.

"Alice," she said. "I won't forget again."

Alice kept walking. Soon she came to a road with two signposts. One sign pointed one way and said TO TWEEDLEDUM'S HOUSE. The other sign pointed the exact same way and said TO THE HOUSE OF TWEEDLEDEE.

"I think they live in the same house!" Alice cried. And she went to go see.

CHAPTER 4

Tweedledum and Tweedledee

～

There they were, standing arm in arm under a tree. They were short, fat men dressed as little boys. Right away, Alice knew which one was which. One had DUM written on his collar. The other had DEE. She assumed they had TWEEDLE in the back, where she couldn't see.

"I know what you're thinking about," the one marked DUM said. "But it isn't so. Nohow."

"Contrairiwise," said the one marked DEE. "If it was so, it might be. And if it were so, it would be. But as it isn't, it ain't. That's logic."

"I was thinking," Alice said politely, "which is the best way out of the woods?"

"Wrong!" Tweedledum cried. "The first thing you say is, 'How d'ye do?' Then shake hands!"

They each held out a hand for her to shake. Alice didn't want to hurt either one's feelings, so she shook both hands at once.

She heard a sound coming from the woods. It sounded like a huge train. Or a wild beast. "Are there any lions or tigers here?" she asked.

"That's only the Red King snoring," Tweedledee said. "Come look at him!" The brothers each took one of Alice's hands and led her to where the King was sleeping.

He slept in red pajamas, snoring loudly.

"He's dreaming now," said Tweedledee. "What do you think he's dreaming about?"

"Nobody can guess that," Alice said.

"He's dreaming about you!" Tweedledee exclaimed. "And if he stopped dreaming about you, where do you think you'd be?"

"Where I am now, of course," Alice said.

"No!" Tweedledee said. "You'd be nowhere. You're only a thing in his dream!"

"If the King were to wake," added Tweedledum, "you'd go out—bang! Just like a candle. You know very well you're not real."

"I *am* real!" Alice said. She began to cry.

"You won't make yourself a bit realer by crying," Tweedledee said.

"If I wasn't real, I shouldn't be able to cry," Alice said. She was half laughing through her tears. It seemed so ridiculous.

"I hope you don't think those are real tears," Tweedledum said.

I know they're talking nonsense, Alice thought. She brushed away her tears.

"I'd better be getting out of the woods," she said as cheerfully as she could. "It's getting dark. Do you think it's going to rain?"

Tweedledum opened a giant umbrella over him and his brother. They both looked up into it. "No, I don't think it is," he said. "At least not under here. Nohow."

"But it may rain *outside*?"

Tweedledee shrugged. "It may, if it chooses. We have no objections."

They stood together under their umbrella. They made no room for Alice.

Selfish things! she thought.

It was getting dark so quickly. Alice thought there must be a thunderstorm on the way. She looked up into the dark sky. "What a thick black cloud that is!" she said. "And look how fast it's coming. I think it's got wings!"

"It's a crow!" the two brothers cried. They dropped their umbrella and ran off into the trees.

Alice ran a little way, too. She stopped to catch her breath under a large tree. "It can never get me *here*," she told herself. "It's far too large to squeeze in under the trees. Still, I wish it wouldn't flap its wings so much. It's so windy. Look—somebody's shawl is being blown away."

CHAPTER 5

Jam Every Other Day

⌒

Alice caught the shawl.

At this moment, the White Queen ran past. Actually, she seemed to be flying. Either way, Alice went to give her the shawl.

The White Queen was dressed crookedly. She had pins stuck all over her clothes, but they weren't holding anything. "May I put your shawl on straight for you?" Alice asked.

"I don't know what's the matter with it," the Queen said sadly. "I've pinned it here, and I've pinned it there. There's no pleasing it."

Alice gently put the shawl on her. "Dear me, what a state your hair is in!" she said.

"The brush got tangled in it," the Queen said with a sigh. "And I lost the comb yesterday."

Alice carefully removed the brush from the Queen's hair. She brushed it as best as she could. "That's better," she said. "But you should really hire a maid to look after you."

"I'll take you with pleasure!" the Queen said. "Two cents a day, and jam every other day."

Alice laughed. "I don't want you to hire *me*. And I don't really want any jam today."

"You couldn't have it if you *did* want it," the Queen said. "The rule is jam tomorrow and jam yesterday. But never jam today."

"It must come sometime," Alice said.

"It can't," the Queen said. "It's jam every *other* day. Today isn't any *other* day."

"How confusing!" Alice said.

"That's how it is when you live backward,"

the Queen said. "But the great advantage is that one's memory works both ways."

"I best remember things that happen the week after next." She put a bandage on her finger. Then she started screaming. "My finger's bleeding!" she cried. "Oh, oh, oh!"

"Did you prick your finger?" Alice asked.

"I haven't pricked it *yet*," the Queen said. "But I will soon. Oh, oh, oh——"

"When do you expect to do it?" Alice asked.

"When I fasten my shawl," the Queen said. "The brooch will come undone." As she said this, her brooch flew open. She clutched at it.

"Be careful!" Alice cried. "You're holding it all crooked!" She tried to grab it out of the Queen's hands, but it was too late. The pin had slipped, and the Queen had pricked her finger.

"That accounts for the bleeding," the Queen said calmly.

The brooch had come undone again. A

sudden gust of wind blew the Queen's shawl across a little brook. She spread out her arms and went flying after it. Somehow she just caught it.

Alice crossed the brook after the Queen. "I hope your finger is better now?" she asked.

"Oh, much better!" the Queen cried. "Much be-etter! Be-etter! Be-e-e-etter! Be-e-ehh!" The last word ended in a bleat, like a sheep.

Alice looked at the Queen. She seemed to have wrapped herself up in wool.

Was that a sheep?

Alice rubbed her eyes.

The next thing she knew, she was standing beside a wall looking up at an enormous egg, with absolutely no idea how she had gotten there.

CHAPTER 6

Humpty Dumpty

⌒

The giant egg had eyes and a nose and a mouth. It was sitting on top of a very high wall. When she came closer, Alice realized it could only be Humpty Dumpty himself. It was just like in the nursery rhyme. She recited it softly to herself:

> Humpty Dumpty sat on a wall:
> Humpty Dumpty had a great fall.
> All the King's horses and all the King's men
> Couldn't put Humpty Dumpty in his place again.

"That last line is too long," she said aloud. She had forgotten that Humpty Dumpty would hear her.

"Don't chatter to yourself like that," Humpty Dumpty said. "Tell me your name and your business."

"My *name* is Alice, but——"

"What a stupid name!" Humpty Dumpty interrupted. "What does it mean?"

"Must a name mean something?" Alice asked.

"Of course it must," Humpty Dumpty said, laughing. "*My* name means the shape I am. And a good, handsome shape, too. With a name like yours, you could be any shape at all."

"Why do you sit out here all alone?" Alice asked. She didn't want to start an argument.

"Why, because there's nobody with me!" cried Humpty Dumpty. "Did you think I didn't know the answer to *that*? Ask another."

"Don't you think it would be safer on the

ground?" Alice asked. She didn't mean it to be a riddle. She was just worried that he would fall over and crack open. "That wall you're on is *very* narrow," she added.

"What easy riddles you ask!" Humpty Dumpty said. "Of course I don't think so! If I ever *did* fall off—which there is no chance of—but *if* I did—" Here he looked very serious. "If I fell, the *King* promised to—"

"To send all of his horses and all of his men," Alice finished. She couldn't help it.

Humpty Dumpty looked shocked and upset. "You've been spying on me!" he cried. "How else could you have known that?"

"No!" Alice protested. "I read it in a book."

This seemed to satisfy Humpty Dumpty. "It must have been a history book," he said. "Take a good look at me: I have spoken to a King!" He grinned proudly from ear to ear.

"What a beautiful belt you've got on!" Alice

said suddenly. She had just noticed the colorful stripe around his waist. Then she had second thoughts. "At least," she said, "a beautiful necktie. Or is it a belt? Oh, I beg your pardon."

Humpty Dumpty looked offended.

If only I knew which was the neck and which was the waist, Alice thought in alarm.

"It is *most upsetting,*" Humpty Dumpty growled, "when someone does not know a necktie from a belt."

"It was very stupid of me," Alice said.

This made Humpty Dumpty less angry. "It's a necktie, dear child. And a beautiful one, as you said. It was a present from the White King and Queen. An un-birthday present."

"What is that?" Alice asked, confused.

"A present given to you when it isn't your birthday. Obviously."

Alice thought about this. "Well, I like birthday presents best," she said.

"You don't know what you're talking about!" yelled Humpty Dumpty. "How many days are there in a year?"

"Three hundred and sixty-five," Alice answered.

"And how many birthdays do you have?"

"One."

"And if you take one from three hundred and sixty-five, what do you have left?"

"Three hundred and sixty-four, of course."

Humpty Dumpty looked doubtful, but Alice assured him her math was correct.

"Well, then," he continued, as if he still didn't quite believe her, "that means there are three hundred and sixty-four days for you to get un-birthday presents. And just *one* for birthday presents. There's *glory* for you!"

Alice shrugged. She still thought birthday presents were far better. She just didn't see the use in arguing about it with an egg.

"I don't know what you mean by *glory*," she said.

Humpty Dumpty sighed. "Of course you don't. I meant, 'There's a nice argument for you.'"

"But *glory* doesn't mean that," Alice said.

"Yes, it does," Humpty Dumpty said. "When *I* use a word, it means what I choose it to mean. Neither more nor less."

Alice was about to argue some more. Then something occurred to her. "You seem very clever about words," she said. "Would you tell me the meaning of the poem 'Jabberwocky'?"

"Let's hear it," Humpty Dumpty said. "I can explain every poem ever invented. And a good many that haven't been invented yet."

This sounded hopeful, so Alice recited the first four lines:

> 'Twas brillig, and the slithy toves
> Did gyre and gimble in the wabe:

All mimsy were the borogoves,

And the mome raths outgrabe.

Humpty Dumpty spoke with a voice of authority. "*Brillig* means four o'clock in the afternoon," he said. "You know, the time when you begin *broiling* things for dinner."

"That makes sense," Alice said. "What about *slithy*?"

"That means *lithe* and *slimy*. *Lithe* is the same as *active*. You see, it's like a suitcase. There are two meanings packed up into one word."

"I see," Alice said. "But what are *toves*?"

"They're something like badgers. And they're something like lizards. And they're something like corkscrews."

"They must be very odd-looking creatures."

"They are," Humpty Dumpty said. "Also they make their nests under sundials. And they live on cheese."

"And what's to *gyre* and to *gimble*?"

"To *gyre* is to go around like a gyroscope. To *gimble* is to make holes like a gimblet."

"And *the wabe* must be the grassy area under the sundial?" Alice asked. She was surprised at how quickly she was picking this up.

"Obviously," Humpty Dumpty said. "And *mimsy* means flimsy and miserable. (That's another suitcase for you.) And a *borogove* is a thin, shabby bird with feathers sticking up all over. It looks something like a living mop."

"And *mome raths*?" said Alice.

"A *rath* is a kind of green pig. But *mome* I'm not sure about. I think it's short for 'from home.' Meaning a green pig that got lost."

"And what does *outgrabe* mean?"

"*Outgrabing* is something between bellowing and whistling, with a kind of sneeze in the middle. You'll hear it in the woods over there. And once you've heard it, you'll be *quite* content."

There was a long pause.

"Is that all?" Alice asked.

"That's all," Humpty Dumpty said. "Good-bye."

This was rather sudden. But after such a strong hint to go, Alice thought it would be hardly polite to stay. She held out her hand. "Good-bye," she said cheerfully. "Until we meet again."

"I wouldn't know you if we *did* meet," Humpty Dumpty said. "You're so exactly like other people."

"The face is what one goes by," Alice said. "Usually."

"That's what I mean," Humpty Dumpty said. "Your face is the same as everybody else's. The two eyes. The nose in the middle. The mouth under it. It's always the same. Now if you had two eyes on the same side of the nose, or the mouth at the top, that would be *some* help."

"That wouldn't look nice," Alice said.

But Humpty Dumpty shut his eyes. "Wait until you've tried it," he said.

She waited a minute to see if he would speak again. But he sat there on top of the wall, his eyes shut tight.

"Good-bye!" she said once more. When she got no answer, she walked away into the woods. "Of all the unsatisfactory people—" she started to say out loud. She liked saying the very long word, but she never got to finish her sentence. At that moment, a very heavy crash shook the forest from end to end.

CHAPTER 7

The Lion and the Unicorn

Soldiers were running through the woods. First in twos and threes, and then in tens and twenties. At last, there were so many, they seemed to fill the whole forest. Alice hid behind a tree.

In all her life, she had never seen soldiers so unsteady on their feet. They were always tripping. And whenever one went down, a few more fell on top of him. Soon the ground was covered in heaps of men.

Then came the horses. They were better than the men, but even they stumbled sometimes.

And it seemed to be a rule that whenever a horse stumbled, the rider fell off.

The confusion was too much. Alice crept away from the woods. Soon she found the White King sitting on the grass writing in his notebook.

The King looked delighted to see her. "Did you happen to meet any soldiers, my dear, when you came through the woods?" he asked.

"Yes, I did," Alice said. "Several thousand."

"Four thousand two hundred and seven," the King said, looking at his notebook. "That's the exact number. I couldn't send all the horses, you know. Two of them are wanted in the game. And I haven't sent the two Messengers, either. They're both going to town. Just look to the road and tell me if you see them."

"I see nobody on the road," Alice said.

"I wish *I* had such eyes," the King said. "To be able to see Nobody! And at that distance, too!"

This was lost on Alice. She was still looking at the road. "I see somebody now!" she cried.

"That's Haigha," the King said. "The other messenger's called Hatta. I have two, you know. One to come, and one to go."

Haigha arrived, quite out breath.

"Whom did you pass on the road?" the King asked him.

"Nobody," said Haigha.

"Quite right," the King said. "This young lady saw him, too. Now tell us what's happened in town."

"I'll whisper it," Haigha said. He put his hands to his mouth in the shape of a trumpet. Then he leaned very close to the King's ear. Alice was sorry about this. She wanted to hear, too. However, instead of whispering, Haigha shouted at the top of his lungs, "They're at it again!"

"You call that a whisper?" the King cried.

"Who are at it again?" Alice asked.

"The Lion and the Unicorn, of course," the King said.

"Fighting for the crown?" Alice asked.

"Yes," the King said. "For *my* crown. Let's run and see them."

As they ran, Alice sang the song:

The Lion and the Unicorn were fighting for the
   crown;
The Lion beat the Unicorn all around the town;
Some gave them white bread, some gave them
   brown;
Some gave them plum cake and drummed them
   out of town.

"Does the one who wins get the crown?" Alice asked.

"No!" the King cried. "What an idea!"

When they reached town, they found a huge crowd. The Lion and the Unicorn were fighting in the middle. They were in such a cloud of dust that Alice could not tell one from the other. Then she was able to pick out the Unicorn by its horn.

They stood near Hatta, the king's other messenger. Hatta was watching the fight with a cup of tea in one hand and a piece of bread and butter in the other.

"How are they doing?" the King asked.

Hatta began to speak, but his mouth was full of bread and butter. He tried desperately to swallow. Finally he said in a choking voice, "They're doing very well. Each of them has been down about eighty-seven times."

The fight paused. The Lion and the Unicorn stood there, panting. "Ten minutes for snacks!" the King called to the crowd. Haigha and Hatta set off with trays of white and brown bread. Alice took a piece, but it was *very* dry.

"I don't think they'll fight any more today. Order the drums to begin," the King told Hatta.

Suddenly Alice saw a streak of white in the distance. "Look!" she cried. "There's the White Queen running across the field! She came out of the woods. How fast those queens can run!"

"There's some enemy after her, no doubt," the King said. He didn't even look. "The woods are full of them."

"Aren't you going to run and help her?" Alice asked.

"No use," the King said. "She runs so fearfully quick. You might as well try to catch a Bander-snatch."

At that moment, the Unicorn walked past. His eyes fell on Alice. He stopped at once, a look of horror on his face. "What is *that*?" he said.

"This is a child!" Haigha cried. "We just found it! It's large as life, and twice as natural!"

"I always thought they were fabulous monsters," the Unicorn said in awe. "Is it alive?"

"It can talk," Haigha said solemnly.

The Unicorn gazed at Alice. "Talk, child."

Alice couldn't help but smile. "You know," she said, "I always thought unicorns were fabulous monsters! I've never seen one before."

"Well, now that we've seen each other, I'll believe in you if you believe in me," the Unicorn said. "Do we have a deal?"

"Of course," Alice said.

"Fetch the plum cake, old man!" the Unicorn yelled at the King. "No brown bread for me."

"Certainly, certainly," the King muttered. He motioned for Haigha to serve the cake.

Haigha took a large cake out of a tiny bag. He gave it to Alice to hold. Then he got out a big dish and a long carving knife. She had no idea how the tiny bag could hold it all. It was like a magic trick.

The Lion joined them for cake as well. He was gazing at Alice, blinking in exhaustion. He seemed very tired. "What is this?" he asked.

"You'll never guess!" the Unicorn said.

"Are you an animal, a vegetable, or a mineral?" the Lion asked Alice.

"It's a fabulous monster!" the Unicorn cried before Alice could answer.

"Then hand out the plum cake, Monster," the Lion said. He lay down on the ground, yawning. "And sit down, the both of you," he called up to the King and the Unicorn.

The King seemed very nervous to sit between the two giant creatures. But there was no other place for him.

"What a fight we could have for the crown now!" the Unicorn said. He looked slyly at the crown on the King's head.

"I'd win, easy," the Lion said.

"I'm not so sure of that," the Unicorn said.

"I beat you all around the town, you chicken!" the Lion snarled angrily.

Here the King interrupted nervously. "All around the town?" he said, his voice shaking a little. "Did you go near the old bridge?"

"I don't remember," the Lion growled. Then he looked over at Alice. "What a time the Monster is having trying to cut that cake!"

Alice had sat down on the bank of a little brook. She had the giant dish on her knees. She was sawing away at the cake with the big knife. "I've cut several slices already," she called. "But they always join back together again."

"You don't know how to handle looking-glass cakes," the Unicorn said. "Hand it around first. Cut it afterward."

This sounded like nonsense. Still, Alice did as he said. The cake divided itself into three slices as she carried it around. Then she held the knife over the empty dish, not sure how to begin.

"It's not fair!" the Unicorn cried. "The Monster has given the Lion a bigger piece!"

"She kept none for herself, though," the Lion said. He turned to Alice. "Monster, don't you like plum cake?"

Before Alice could answer, the drums began. The noise filled the air. It rang though her head until she thought she might go deaf. She jumped across the little brook in terror. She covered her ears. The noise was more than she could bear.

CHAPTER 8

The Great Art of Riding

~

After a while, the noise died down. Alice looked up. She was surprised to find herself alone with the giant dish that had held the plum cake at her feet.

A Red Knight galloped toward her. "Check!" the Red Knight cried. "You're my prisoner!" Then he fell off his horse.

As he climbed back on the horse, another shout was heard. "Ahoy, ahoy! Check!"

Alice looked around in surprise for the new enemy. It was a White Knight. He stopped beside Alice, fell off his horse, got back on again, and then sat there staring at the Red Knight. Alice looked from one to the other in confusion.

"She's *my* prisoner," the Red Knight said.

"Yes, but then I came and rescued her," the White Knight said.

"Well, we must fight for her, then," the Red Knight said.

"You will observe the rules of battle?" the White Knight asked.

"I always do," the Red Knight replied.

The knights faced off. They fell off their horses onto their heads. They got on again. They fell off again. They got on again, and then the battle seemed to be over. They shook hands, and the Red Knight rode away.

"A glorious victory, wasn't it?" the White Knight called to Alice. He was quite out of breath.

"I don't know," Alice said. "But I don't want to be anyone's prisoner. I want to be a queen."

"So you will be when you cross the next

brook," the White Knight said. "I'll see you safe to the edge of the woods. Then I must go back. That's the end of my move."

"Thank you very much," Alice said.

They headed toward the brook. The Knight rode his horse, and Alice walked at his side. The only problem was that the Knight wasn't a very good rider. He kept falling off the horse, and Alice kept helping him back up.

"I'm afraid you haven't had much practice in riding," Alice said. She had just helped him up from his fifth tumble.

"I've had plenty of practice!" the Knight cried. "The art of great riding is to keep—" The Knight fell off the horse onto his head.

Alice was startled. She picked him up. "I hope no bones were broken?" she said.

"None to speak of," said the Knight, as if he didn't mind breaking two or three. "The great art of riding is to keep your balance. Like this."

He stretched out both his arms. This time, he fell flat on his back under the horse's feet.

"Plenty of practice!" he said as Alice helped him up yet again.

"It's ridiculous," Alice said. "You should get a wooden horse on wheels."

"Does that kind go smoothly?" the Knight asked. He seemed deeply interested.

"Much more smoothly than a live horse," Alice said.

"I'll get one," the Knight said to himself. Then he turned his horse and said to Alice, "You have only a few yards to go. Down the hill and over the brook. Then you'll be a queen. . . . But you'll

see me off first? You'll wave a handkerchief when I reach the turn in the road?"

Alice looked eagerly down the hill toward the brook. She was desperate to finish her journey, but she couldn't make the Knight unhappy. "Of course I'll wait," she told him.

They shook hands, and the Knight headed off into the forest. He tumbled off the horse—first on one side, then on the other. She waved her handkerchief until he was out of sight.

Then she turned and ran down the hill. "To be a queen!" she cried as she ran. "How grand it sounds!" A very few steps brought her to the edge of the brook. "The Eighth Square at last!" she cried as she leaped across.

Alice threw herself down among the flower beds. "Oh, how glad I am to be here!" she said. "And what *is* that on my head?" It was something heavy and tight. She pulled it off.

It was a golden crown.

CHAPTER 9

Queen Alice

⚬

"Well, this *is* grand!" Alice said as she placed the crown back on her head. "I never expected to be a queen so soon! And I'll tell you what, Your Majesty," she went on. Her voice had turned serious. She always did like to scold herself. "You should not be lolling around in the grass like that. Queens must be dignified."

She stood up and walked around. She was careful not to let the crown fall off. "If I really am a queen, I should be able to manage it quite well in time," she said. That made her feel better.

When she sat down again she was not at all surprised that the Red Queen and the White Queen were sitting with her. She wondered if this meant the game was now over. She turned to the Red Queen and said, "Please, would you tell me—"

"Speak when you're spoken to!" the Red Queen roared.

"But if everybody did that, if you always waited to be spoken to, and if the other person always waited for *you* to speak first, nobody would ever say anything—"

"Ridiculous!" the Red Queen yelled. But she sat there thinking about it for a minute. She had no other argument.

"What did you mean by 'If I really am a queen'?" the Red Queen asked. "What right do you have to call yourself that? You can't be a queen, you know, until you pass the test."

"I only said 'if'!" Alice protested.

The two queens looked at each other. "Always speak the truth. Think before you speak. And write it down afterward," the Red Queen said.

"I didn't mean——" Alice started to explain.

"Exactly!" the Red Queen shrieked. "What is the use of a child without meaning?" Then the Red Queen turned to the White Queen. "I invite you to Alice's dinner party this afternoon."

The White Queen smiled. "And I invite *you.*"

"I didn't know I was having a party," Alice said. "But if there is going to be one, I think *I* should invite the guests."

"We gave you the chance to do it," the Red Queen said. "You haven't had many classes in manners yet, have you?"

"Manners are not taught in class," Alice said. "In class, you learn math and that sort of thing."

"Can you do addition?" the White Queen

asked. "What's one and one and one and one and one and one and one and one and one?"

"I don't know," Alice said. "I lost count."

"She can't do addition," the Red Queen said.

"Can *you* do addition?" Alice asked, turning to the White Queen.

The White Queen gasped and shut her eyes. "I can do addition," she said. "If you give me time. But not subtraction under *any* circumstances."

"Of course you know your ABCs," the Red Queen said to Alice.

"I do," Alice said.

"Can you answer the useful questions?" the Red Queen said. "How is bread made?"

"You take some flour—" Alice began.

"Where do you pick the flower?" the White Queen asked. "In the garden or in the hedges?"

"It isn't *picked*," Alice said. "It's ground—"

"How many acres of ground?" the White

Queen said. "You shouldn't leave out so many things."

"Fan her head!" the Red Queen interrupted. "She'll be feverish after so much thinking."

They fanned Alice with leaves.

"She's all right again," the Red Queen said. "Do you know languages?" she asked Alice. "What's French for 'fiddle-dee-dee'?"

"'Fiddle-dee-dee is not English,'" Alice said.

"Who ever said it was?" the Red Queen asked.

Alice tried to think of a way out of this. "If you tell me what language 'fiddle-dee-dee' is, I'll tell you the French for it."

"Queens don't make bargains," the Red Queen said, sitting up stiffly.

I wish queens didn't ask questions, Alice thought.

The White Queen sighed. She put her head on Alice's shoulder. "I am so sleepy!" she moaned.

"She's tired, poor thing!" the Red Queen said. "Smooth her hair. Sing her a lullaby."

"I don't know any," Alice said.

"I must do it myself, then," the Red Queen said. And she began:

Hush-a-bye, lady, in Alice's lap!
Till the feast's ready, we have time for a nap.
When the feast's over, we'll go to the ball—
Red Queen and White Queen and Alice and all!

"Now you know the words," the Red Queen said. "So sing it to *me*. I'm getting sleepy, too." She put her head on Alice's other shoulder.

In another moment, both Queens were asleep.

"What *am* I to do?" Alice said. The Queens' heads rolled onto her lap. "I don't think this has ever happened before, that anyone had to take care of two sleeping Queens at once! Do wake up, heavy things!"

The Queens were snoring. It sounded like a song. Alice tried to make out the words. She was listening so closely that when the heads vanished from her lap, she didn't even miss them.

Alice looked up and saw a doorway nearby. She walked up to it. Over the door were the words QUEEN ALICE. There were two bells. One was marked VISITORS' BELL and the other was marked SERVANTS' BELL.

"I'm not a visitor," Alice said to herself. "And I'm not a servant. One of the bells should say QUEEN."

Just then the door opened. A creature with a long beak poked its head out. "No one can come in until the week after next," it said, and shut the door again with a bang.

She knocked and knocked on the door, but there was no answer. A very old frog was sitting under a tree. He got up and walked toward Alice. "What is it?" he asked.

"Where's the person who should answer this door?" she asked angrily.

"Which door?" said the Frog.

"This door, of course!"

The Frog looked at the door. Then he went closer and poked at it with his thumb. Then he looked back to Alice. "To answer the door?" he said. "What has it been asking?"

"I don't know what you mean."

"It speaks English, doesn't it? Or are you deaf? What did it ask you?"

"Nothing! I've been knocking on it!"

"You shouldn't do that," the Frog said. "It bothers it. You let *it* alone, and it will let *you* alone." Then he hobbled back to his tree.

Suddenly, the door flew open. There was a chorus of cheers. Alice went inside. But as soon as she did, there was dead silence.

She saw a large table in a great hall. Sitting at

the table were about fifty guests of all kinds: some animals, some birds, and even a few flowers. There were three chairs at the head of the table. The Red Queen and the White Queen had already taken two of them. The middle one was empty, so Alice sat in it.

At last the Red Queen spoke. "You missed the soup and the fish," she said. "Give her some mutton!" The waiters brought Alice a leg of mutton. She looked at it anxiously. She had no idea what to do with it.

"You look a little shy," the Red Queen said. "Let me introduce you. Alice, Mutton. Mutton, Alice." The leg of mutton got up on the dish and bowed. Alice bowed, too. She didn't know if she should be scared or amused.

Alice lifted her fork. "May I give you a slice?" she asked the Queens.

"Certainly not!" the Red Queen said. "It isn't

very polite to cut some-
one you've just been
introduced to! Remove
the mutton!" The wait-
ers carried it off.

"Let's drink to your
health," the Red Queen
cried. "To Queen Alice's health!" she screamed.

The guests began drinking whatever was in
their glasses. They did it however they could, and
quite oddly. Some of them dumped their glasses
on their heads and drank as it trickled down their
faces. Others knocked their glasses over and
drank the spills off the table.

"You should give a speech," the Red Queen
told Alice.

"We must support you, you know," the White
Queen whispered.

Alice stood up nervously. The Red Queen and

the White Queen pushed on her—supporting her, even though she didn't need it. They pushed so much, they almost squeezed her flat.

In fact, it was difficult to keep standing. The two Queens almost lifted her up into the air as she spoke. "I rise to give thanks—" Alice said. She really *was* rising now, several inches off the ground. Finally she was able to pull herself down.

"Take care of yourself!" the White Queen screamed. She grabbed Alice's hair. "Something's going to happen!" she cried.

And then all sorts of things began to happen.

The candles grew up to the ceiling. The bottles each took a pair of plates and attached them like wings, took forks for legs, and started fluttering around through the air.

Alice heard a rough laugh at her side. She thought at first it was the White Queen, but it was the leg of mutton.

"Here I am!" Alice heard. She turned just in time to see the White Queen grinning at her from the soup bowl. Then she disappeared inside.

Many of the guests were lying down in the dishes. The soup ladle was walking up toward Alice, motioning for her to get out of her seat.

"I can't stand this anymore!" Alice cried. She grabbed the tablecloth with both hands. With one good pull, the plates, glasses, guests, and candles came crashing down into a heap on the floor.

"And as for *you*," Alice said, turning to the Red Queen. Alice was sure it was all her fault. But the Red Queen was no longer beside her. She had shrunk to the size of a small doll. She was now on the table chasing her own shawl around in circles.

At any other time, Alice would have been surprised at this. But she was far too excited to be surprised by anything now.

"As for *you*," she repeated, catching hold of the little creature, "I'll shake you into a kitten, I will!"

CHAPTER 10

Who Dreamed It?

Alice took the tiny Red Queen off the table and shook her with all her might. She shook her backward. She shook her forward.

The Red Queen's face got small. And her eyes got large and green. And still, as Alice went on shaking her, she kept changing. She got shorter. And fatter. And rounder. And . . .

. . . it really *was* a kitten after all!

"Your Red Majesty shouldn't purr so loudly," Alice told her fuzzy black kitten. "You woke me out of such a nice dream! And you were there with me, Kitty. Did you know?"

It is a very bothersome habit of kittens, Alice thought, that no matter what you say to them, they always purr. There is no way to tell a yes from a no.

So Alice hunted around among the chess pieces until she found the Red Queen. She held it out before the kitten. "Now, Kitty," she said, "confess that this is what you turned into!"

But the kitten wouldn't confess.

"Now, Kitty," Alice continued, "let's consider who it was who dreamed it all. You see, Kitty, it must have been either me or the Red King. He was part of my dream, but then I was part of his dream, too! *Was* it the Red King, Kitty? You were the Red Queen, so you really should know. Oh, Kitty, please tell me!"

But the kitten only began licking her paw, pretending it didn't hear the question.

Who do *you* think it was?

What Do *You* Think?
Questions for Discussion

⌒

Have you ever been around a toddler who keeps asking the question "Why?" all the time? Does your teacher call on you in class with questions from your homework? Do your parents ask you questions about your day at the dinner table? We are always surrounded by questions that need a specific response. But is it possible to have a question with no right answer?

The following questions are about the book you just read. But this is not a quiz! They are designed to help you look at the people, places, and events in the story from different angles. These questions do not have specific answers. Instead, they might make you think of the story in a completely new way.

Think carefully about each question and enjoy discovering more about this classic story.

1. How does Alice react the first time she sees the White Rabbit? What would you have done in her place?

2. The narrator says that Alice likes to pretend to be two people. Why do you suppose this is? What do you pretend when you play?

3. Alice continues to alternate between being big and small. What are the benefits of each one? Which would you prefer?

4. Alice says, "I've seen a cat without a grin, but a grin without a cat! That's the most curious thing I've ever seen in my life." What is the most curious thing *you've* ever seen?

5. Alice says of the poem *Jabberwock,* "It seems very pretty . . . but it is *very* hard to understand." What does Humpty Dumpty tell her it means? Were you able to make any sense of it?

6. The flowers say that it isn't good manners for them to speak first. Do you agree? Do you have good manners?

7. Why do you suppose the gnat keeps whispering jokes in Alice's ear? Do you like to tell jokes? What's your best one?

8. Humpty Dumpty and Alice argue about whether they prefer birthdays or unbirthdays. Which would you prefer to celebrate?

9. Many of the characters in Alice's dreams represent people in her real life. Which character are you the most like? Which are you the least like?

10. Were you surprised to find out that Alice's experiences were only dreams? Do you remember your dreams? What is the most unusual one you can recall?

Afterword
By *Arthur Pober, Ed.D.*

⌒

First impressions are important.

Whether we are meeting new people, going to new places, or picking up a book unknown to us, first impressions count for a lot. They can lead to warm, lasting memories or can make us shy away from any future encounters.

Can you recall your own first impressions and earliest memories of reading the classics?

Do you remember wading through pages and pages of text to prepare for an exam? Or were you the child who hid under the blanket to read with a flashlight, joining forces with Robin Hood to save Maid Marian? Do you remember only how long it took you to read a lengthy novel such as *Little Women*? Or did you become best friends with the March sisters?

Even for a gifted young reader, getting through long chapters with dense language can easily become overwhelming and can obscure the richness of the story and its characters. Reading an abridged, newly crafted version of a classic novel can be the gentle introduction a child needs to explore the characters and story-line without the frustration of difficult vocabulary and complex themes.

Reading an abridged version of a classic novel gives the young reader a sense of independence and the satisfaction of finishing a "grown-up" book. And when a child is engaged with and inspired by a classic story, the tone is set for further exploration of the story's themes, characters, history, and details. As a child's reading skills advance, the desire to tackle the original, unabridged version of the story will naturally emerge.

If made accessible to young readers, these stories can become invaluable tools for understanding themselves in the context of their families and social environments. This is why the Classic Starts series includes questions that stimulate discussion regarding the impact and social relevance of the characters and stories today. These questions can foster lively conversations between children and their parents or teachers. When we look at the issues, values, and standards of past times in terms of how we live now, we can appreciate literature's classic tales in a very personal and engaging way.

Share your love of reading the classics with a young child, and introduce an imaginary world real enough to last a lifetime.

Dr. Arthur Pober, Ed.D.

Dr. Arthur Pober has spent more than twenty years in the fields of early childhood and gifted education. He is the former principal of one of the world's oldest laboratory schools for gifted youngsters, Hunter College Elementary School, and former Director of Magnet Schools for the Gifted and Talented for more than 25,000 youngsters in New York City.

Dr. Pober is a recognized authority in the areas of media and child protection and is currently the U.S. representative to the European Institute for the Media and European Advertising Standards Alliance.